What a Day!

Story by Carmel Reilly
Illustrations by Rob Mancini

Contents

Chapter 1

Off We Go!

Kayla, Joe, Mum and Dad
were going on a camping holiday.

Dad said they needed to set off after breakfast.
But it was nearly lunchtime,
and they were still getting ready.

"Don't forget we have to take Mip to the pet hotel before we go," said Kayla.

"That won't take long," said Dad.

11:45

But leaving Mip at the pet hotel was not going to be quick.

Mum had to fill in lots of forms. Then, Dad had to talk to someone about Mip's food for the next week.

"It's getting late," said Kayla, looking at the clock in the office.

"Yes, we should be going," said Dad.

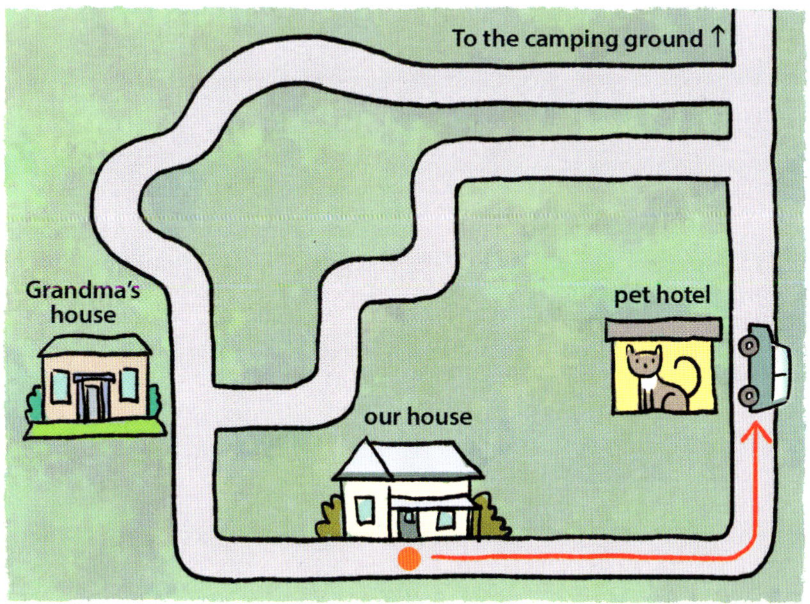

They had just left the pet hotel
when Mum's phone rang.
It was Grandma.
She had locked herself out of her house.

"It's lucky I have another key
to Grandma's house in my bag," said Mum.
"We need to go to her place and let her in.
It won't take long."

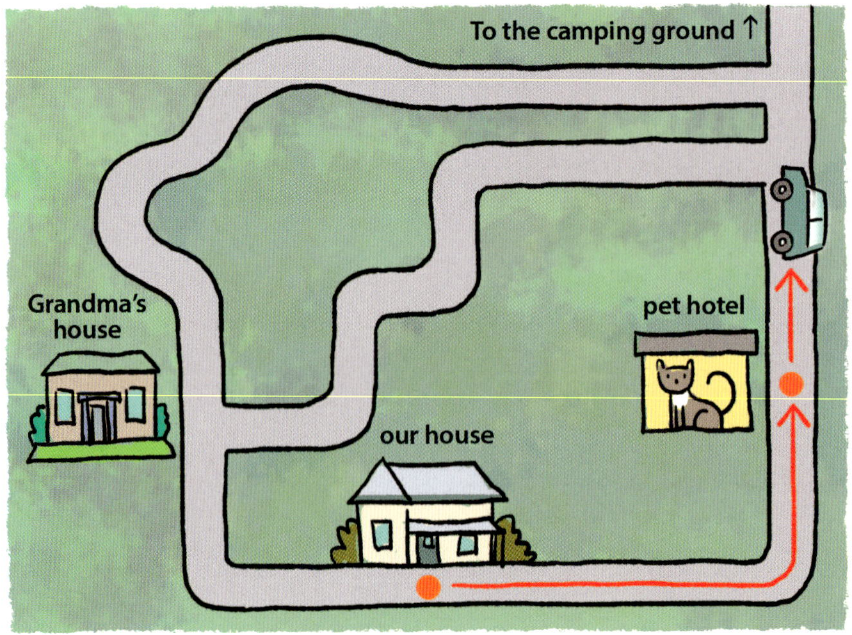

Chapter 2

A Long Lunch

Grandma was waiting at the door.

"I'm so glad you were still around to let me in. You must stay for lunch," she said.

"We don't have a lot of time," said Mum.

"But you need to eat something before you go on that long drive," said Grandma.

"I'm hungry!" said Joe.

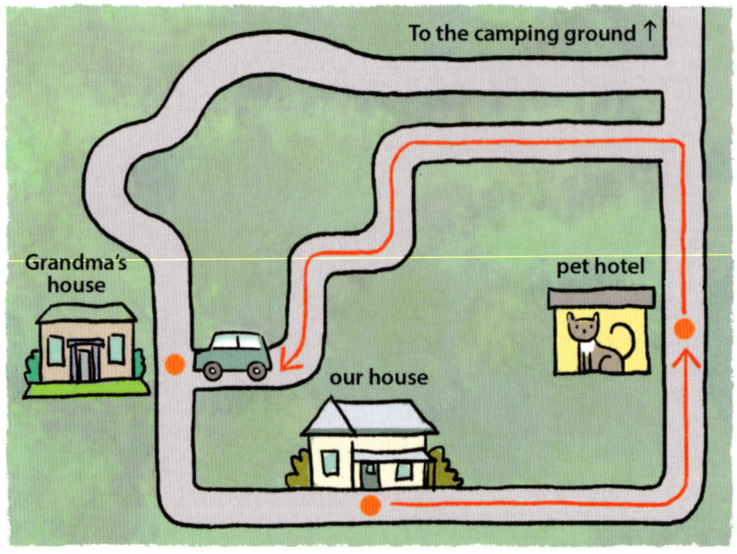

At lunch, they had sandwiches, fruit and some of Grandma's delicious cake. Grandma told them all about the new book she was reading.

Then, she said to Mum and Dad, "Would you like a cup of tea?"

"Yes, please," said Dad.

"But don't we have to get to the camping ground before it gets dark?" asked Kayla.

"We will have time," said Dad.

At last, they were in the car
and on the main road out of town.

“Will we get to the camping ground soon?”
asked Kayla.

“As long as we don’t have to stop again,”
said Dad, with a laugh.

Just then, Mum said,
“Has anyone seen my bag?”

“You had it at Grandma’s place,” said Kayla.

“Oh, no!” said Joe.

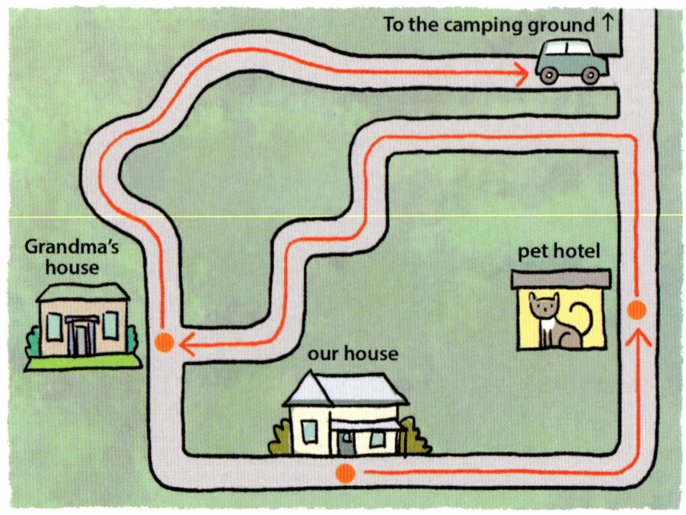

Chapter 3

The Last Stop

Back at Grandma's place,
Kayla found Mum's bag under the table.

"Can you find the email from the camping ground with their phone number?" said Mum. "I'll call them to say we won't come today."

Kayla pulled out the email
and began to read it.
“It’s Wednesday today, isn’t it?” she said.

“Yes,” said Mum. “Why?”

“Well, it says here we are not booked in
until Thursday,” said Kayla.

“Oh, dear,” said Mum. “I mixed up the days!”

“So we are not going to be late after all!” said Kayla.

“Oh, good!” said Grandma.
“Now you can stay for dinner.”